This book belongs to

· · · · · · · · · · · · · · · · · ·

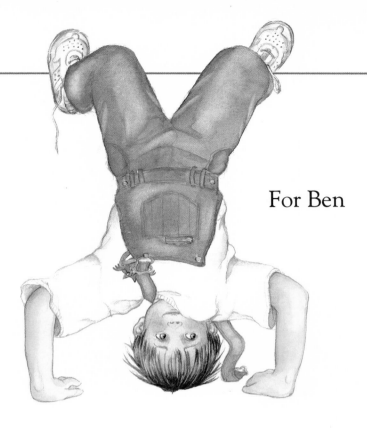

For Ben

A DORLING KINDERSLEY BOOK

First published in Great Britain in 1993
by Dorling Kindersley Limited,
9 Henrietta Street, London WC2E 8PS

Reprinted 1993

A CIP catalogue record for this book is available from the British Library
ISBN 0-7513-7001-0

Colour reproduction by Dot Gradations
Printed in Belgium by Proost

I CAN

SUSAN WINTER

DORLING KINDERSLEY

London • New York • Stuttgart

My sister wants to do whatever I do.

I can dress myself.

She can't.

I can feed myself.

She can't.

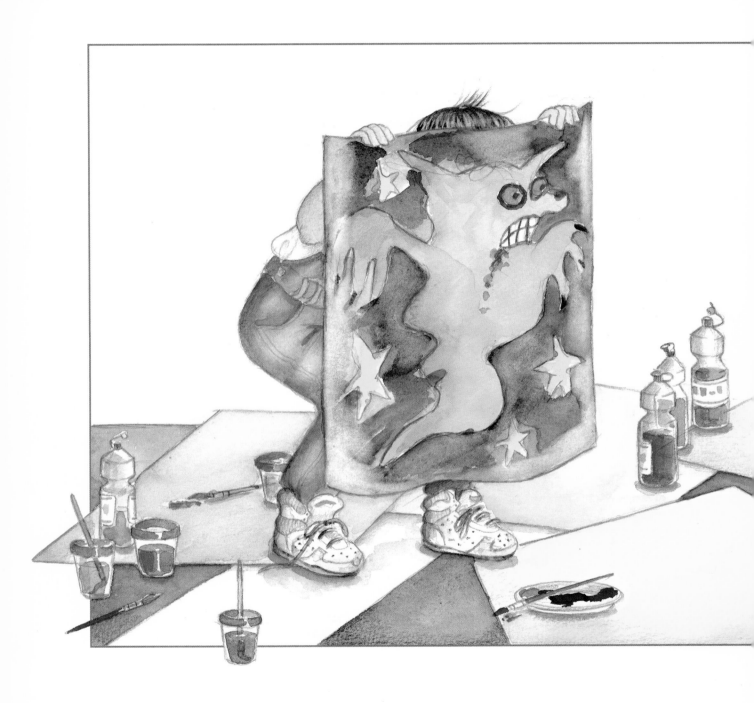

I can paint pictures.

She can't.

I can swim without armbands.

She can't.

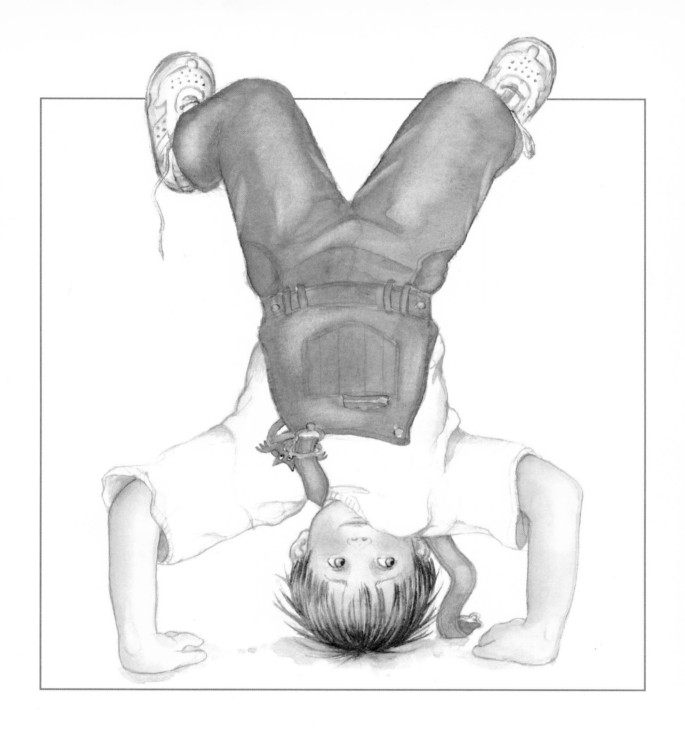

I can stand on my head.

She can't.

I can ride really fast.

She can't.

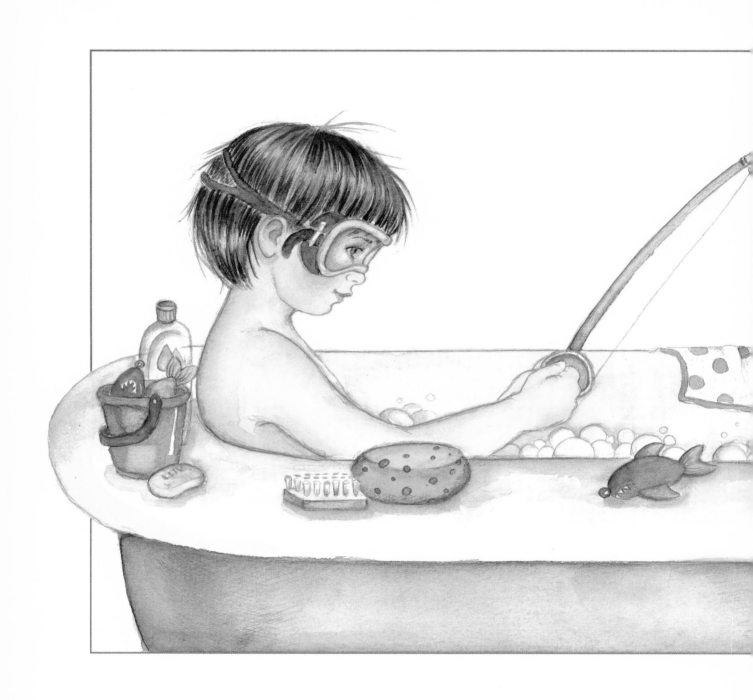

I can bath myself.

She can't.

I can climb into bed.

She can't.

I can see monsters in the dark.

She can't.

She needs me.